A Gift for Goose

To Joanna B. Hills—a gift to many

All rights reserved. Published in the United States by Schwartz & Wade Books, an imprint of Random House Children's Books, a division of Penguin Random House LLC, New York.

Visit us on the Web!
rhcbooks.com

Educators and librarians, for a variety of teaching tools, visit us at RHTeachersLibrarians.com

Library of Congress Cataloging-in-Publication Data is available upon request.
ISBN 978-0-525-64489-7 (hardback) — ISBN 978-0-525-64491-0 (glb)
ISBN 978-0-525-64492-7 (ebook) — ISBN 978-0-525-64490-3 (pbk.)

The text of this book is set in 24-point Century.
The illustrations were rendered in colored pencils and acrylic paint.

MANUFACTURED IN CHINA

2 4 6 8 10 9 7 5 3 1

Duck & Goose

A Gift for Goose

Tad Hills

schwartz & wade books · new york

Duck has a gift
for Goose.

He puts it in a box.

He closes the box.

He paints it red,
yellow, and blue.

He waits
for the paint
to dry.

Duck makes a card.

He puts a blue ribbon
on the box.

"What is that?"
Goose honks.

"It is a gift for you,"
Duck quacks.

"For *me*?
Thank you!
It is the nicest box
I have ever seen!"
honks Goose.

"But . . . ," Duck quacks.

"I can put my special
things in the box,"
Goose honks.

"But . . . ," Duck quacks.

"I will go and get
my special things,"
honks Goose.

"But . . . wait,"
Duck quacks.

Goose gets his crayons,

his shell,

and his winter hat
and scarf.

He gets his summer hat

and his ball of yarn

to put in the box.

"But, Goose,"
Duck says.
"This box is not
your gift."

"What?" honks Goose.

"It is not mine?"

"No. Your gift is *inside*
this box,"
Duck quacks.

Goose opens the box.

He looks inside.

Goose pulls out a
polka-dotted box.
"It is a box! I love it!"
he honks.

"It is for your special
things," quacks Duck.

"Thank you, Duck. It is
the nicest box I have
ever seen!" honks Goose.